PHINEAS THE FOX GROWS A SALSA GARDEN

Written and illustrated by

Nicole Hanson

A Phineas the Fox Story

PHINEAS THE FOX GROWS A SALSA GARDEN

HONEY BIRCH PRESS

For more information, contact us at
www.NicoleHansonArt.com

Print: ISBN/SKU:979-8-3305-1672-8

Phineas was a young fox who lived in the forest with his Momma, Poppa, and brother Oliver.

One morning, Phineas looked at his breakfast.

"Where's Grandpa's salsa?" he asked. It was the best salsa Phineas had ever tasted, and the only way he ate his eggs.

"There's more in the cabinet," Momma said.

Phineas climbed a stool and searched the cabinet.

"Only one jar left?" Phineas said. He grabbed it carefully.

"Wow, I didn't think we'd go through them so fast," said Poppa, bringing Momma her fried eggs.

"I'll add salsa to the grocery list," said Momma.

"Store-bought salsa won't taste like Grandpa's!" Phineas complained.

“You could eat the eggs plain,” said Poppa. Phineas tried a bite of plain eggs.

He decided eggs were better with salsa.

“I guess I’ll have the store-bought salsa,” Phineas said quietly.

Later that day, Poppa showed Phineas an index card.

“Phineas,” said Poppa, “this is your grandpa’s salsa recipe.”

Phineas looked at the index card.

At the bottom, Grandpa had written, “Best with homegrown vegetables!”

"Could we grow a garden like Grandpa's?" Phineas asked, getting excited. "We could make his salsa!"

"It would be your responsibility," said Momma. "But we could help sometimes. And we will help you make the salsa."

Phineas jumped off the couch and danced with excitement.

He would get to eat more of Grandpa’s salsa after all!

Phineas got to work.

One day, the sun felt especially hot on Phineas's back as he lugged the watering can into the garden.

Bugs buzzed in his ears. The garden wasn't fun anymore.

He left the watering can where it was and ran back inside.

“You finished your garden work quickly today,” said Momma. She had nearly finished sweeping the floor.

Phineas didn’t answer.

The garden would be fine without him.

A week later, Phineas sat at the breakfast table. The hot, angry sun rose outside, and Phineas wanted to avoid it.

He would stay inside today. Again.

He hadn't worked in the garden all week.

"If you keep ignoring the garden," said Momma, "it will not produce enough vegetables to make salsa."

"It'll be fine," said Phineas, accidentally bumping the last jar of salsa.

It toppled to the floor.

The glass jar shattered.

Salsa splattered everywhere.

“Oh no!” yelled Phineas.

“Stay in your chair,” said Poppa.
“I'll clean it up.”

“But that was the last jar of
Grandpa's salsa!” said Phineas.

"Here, try the store-bought salsa," said Momma. He tasted it, then made a face.

"It tastes nothing like Grandpa's salsa."

He looked at his brother. Oliver had never even tasted eggs with salsa.

And he never would, unless Phineas could copy Grandpa's salsa.

Phineas scarfed down the rest of the eggs and store-bought salsa.

"Where are you going in such a rush?" asked Poppa.

"The garden," said Phineas.

Phineas marched into the garden, prepared to do the work this time.

Oliver would taste Grandpa's salsa even if it meant a summer of sunburns, bug bites, and prickles in his paws!

The weeds had grown huge and thorny. Phineas dug at them with his shovel.

He swatted mosquitos and brushed away gnats while he worked.

Little by little, he could see his progress.

“Want some help?” asked Momma. “Oliver is napping.”

“Yes! Thank you!”

Phineas and Momma worked together until they reached the last corner of the garden.

They pulled the weeds, watered the plants, and took the pesky hornworms off the branches.

The plants grew and grew.

And grew!

A few weeks later, Phineas jumped out of bed. Grandpa's ingredients would be ripe soon.

Maybe even today!

He ran outside before brushing his teeth and combing his fur. He even ran outside before eating his breakfast.

Could it be salsa day?

He checked under every leaf, but the tomatoes were still green. He needed them to be red before he could make them into salsa.

The garden just wasn't ready yet.

Salsa day would be soon.

At least, he hoped it would. So he and Oliver could both try it.

SALSA!

"You didn't go straight to the garden this morning," said Poppa after breakfast a few days later.

"Is everything all right?" asked Momma.

"What if the garden is never ready?" Phineas asked.

"Would it help if we all went out together?" Poppa suggested.

Phineas nodded. How much longer could he handle the suspense? How much longer until he could eat his grandpa's salsa?

The family walked out to the garden.

Phineas held his breath.

From the door, Phineas could see spots of bright red in the garden.

The tomatoes were ready!
It was salsa day!

Phineas sprinted to the garden, jumping and shouting for joy.

"It's salsa day! It's finally salsa day!"

Together, the family harvested the red, ripe tomatoes and other vegetables.

They carefully followed the directions on Grandpa's recipe and finally made more of the delicious salsa.

"Oliver," Phineas said, "this is Grandpa's salsa."

MORE PHINEAS

Want free coloring pages, Wonderful Salsa recipe, color by numbers, mazes and more?

Go to:

www.NicoleHansonArt.com/garden

There, you will also find an opportunity to purchase a larger resource pack including sorting, sequencing, writing, coloring, punctuation, and feelings activity sheets.

ABOUT NICOLE HANSON

Nicole Hanson grew up telling bedtime stories to her sister, asking family members what she should draw, and writing a novel in the afternoons.

Nicole earned her B.S. in Elementary Education in 2013.

Nicole lives in Minnesota with her husband. She can be found online at NicoleHansonArt.com.

A WORD FROM THE AUTHOR

Your voice matters!

If you enjoyed this book, it would mean the world to me if you would take a minute to leave a heartfelt review on Amazon.

Your kind feedback is very appreciated and helps others know if this book is a good fit for them.

Thank you so much for your time.

Nicole Hanson

Milton Keynes UK
Ingram Content Group UK Ltd.
UKRC031637151124
2882UKWH00044B/150

* 9 7 9 8 3 3 0 5 1 6 7 2 8 *